Whispers from the Past
By
A.J. Hurley

Table of Contents

Chapter 1 4

Chapter 2 8

Chapter 3 13

Chapter 4 19

Chapter 5 22

Chapter 6 25

Chapter 7 30

Chapter 8 34

Chapter 9 40

Chapter 10 43

Chapter 11 51

Chapter 12 59

Chapter 13 67

Chapter 14 72

Author's Note 74

Chapter 1

Dean wasn't sure whether he had enjoyed middle school or not. There had been many bonuses. For one thing, he was a popular lad with lots of good friends with whom he had enjoyed breaks and lunchtimes. And, of course, there was the football. Football was Dean's passion – he could outrun anyone and as an attacking midfielder he had a scoring rate second to none. Whenever he wore the school colours he was transported into another world – a world where he didn't get told off for talking, a world where he was able to demonstrate his ability out of the classroom. It was the lessons that were the trouble – Dean never managed to retain his concentration for long enough to make the 'recommended – or expected – levels of progress'. It made no sense to him. After all, kids weren't like sausage meat, were they? They didn't all do the same things at the same time in the same way. It was like football where everyone did the same drills but, no matter how often they were shown Jonesy and Wilko would miss the goal on every single occasion. Some kids just shouldn't have been on a football pitch.

September came and with it a move to the local secondary school. Mum had taken Dean to the shops and bought him a complete uniform. Although she said that she had something in her eye, Dean was sure Mum cried when she saw him completely kitted out in blazer with badge, crisp white shirt, school trousers, boring grey socks, school tie and shiny black shoes. He thought he looked ridiculous. Style had always been one of Dean's strong points. He was the one with the deliberately untucked sports shirt. His was the hair with exactly the right amount of gel so that it still looked cool but not too over the top. Now he was going to look exactly like all of the others. Dorksville here I come he thought, scowling at his image in the mirror as his mother, grandmother and the shop assistant huddled together conspiratorially. Only Joe, his younger brother knew what he was going through and threw Dean a sympathetic glance. Joe realised, of course, that in two years time it would be his turn and he was making sure that when the time came Dean would share his pain.

The first week went by in a haze of timetables, new lessons, introductions to new teachers and something called 'the Furzedale Way' involving an aspirational motto and a code of conduct. Dean didn't care much for either. How, when you were Dean Wilkins, were you meant to avoid talking for a whole hour? Why did your writing have to be neat, be underlined, and why did presentation matter anyway – surely it was what you wrote not how you wrote it? Sadly Dean's ideas were not in alignment with those of most of the staff and within a few weeks he had gained a reputation for spending more time in the corridors than in lessons. Out in the corridor he could dream of playing for United; he could relive his goals and plan how he was going to play on Saturday.

'Dean, are you listening?'

'Er … what Miss?'

'What page are we on?'

'Haven't got a clue!' Dean would smirk at this point – and it was this tendency to smile, at exactly the wrong moment, that had got him into so much trouble. If the truth were known, Dean Wilkins was not a bad boy; he didn't go out of his way to look for trouble in the middle of a lesson. It was just that nothing really gripped him. He didn't dislike the teachers, although they seemed to dislike him for some reason, but he just didn't get why they needed so much of his attention all of the time. English was just reading and writing, wasn't it? So why did the English teacher seem to turn a peculiar shade of purple when she caught him reading his football annual under the desk? After all he was reading, wasn't he? He betted that she wouldn't have had a chance of telling the class which young Premiership Manager had won

Premiership Manager of the Month three times in a row last season. Just because the class were reading a novel about a family in France who were waiting for someone or other to return home didn't mean he couldn't just listen for a short while and then be able to catch up on the plot for goodness sake!

Drama and reading play scripts aloud were okay. Dean had perfected a mean Scottish accent and could pretend to be a famous often remembered Premiership Manager in almost every situation. There was the time when his star player turned up late to training; the time when someone in the changing room argued with him; the time when the manager had to congratulate his team on winning the Premiership. Dean had a scenario for every situation – anger, excitement, fear, respect, glory – the list went on and on. But now, for some completely inexplicable reason, the English teacher, a middle aged blonde woman, who, when looking at Dean, appeared and sounded as though she had sucked on a lemon covered in curry powder said she found his scenarios somewhat lacking in scope and development. What did she know? She wouldn't last five minutes as a football coach! What about enthusiasm and looking for individual flair and development? No, Dean reasoned, the whole school system was biased against free thinking, against free spirited individuals like him.

'So, Dean, can you explain the boy in the story's motivation for helping Jewish children to escape across the border?'

'No not really miss. Now if it were a football manager arranging a free transfer for a player who had caused grief, then I could understand the logic. As for that boy in the story, though, well, no. Why would anybody put themselves in that much danger? I mean would you? We'd all like to say we would and that we were brave and all that – but honestly? Knowing that you and your family would most probably be killed – would you really do this?'

By now there were sundry individual conversations going on around the class – clearly not something that the teacher had planned. Her face was, Dean thought to himself, an interesting colour – somewhere between the red of Manchester United and the purple of West Ham – and she looked for all the world as though her eyes were going to pop out of her head.

'Enough!' the teacher finally half screamed and half shouted. 'This is NOT a lesson about football. It is not now and never will be about football. It is about understanding the reasons why people write about different things so that people like us can stand here and discuss what's important'.

The boy at the back of the class, another feisty young man, said 'Well Miss if you look at the money made by the Premiership – and by Premiership footballers for that matter – we could have a whole class discussion about it.'

This was apparently the last straw. The teacher sent out the boy – George – and gave Dean the death stare as if to suggest that it was all his fault. It always was, it seemed. Dean would never understand exactly why it was that teachers were so intransigent. Didn't they expect their pupils to be able to adapt to five or six different subjects and skills in a day? Why did a simple, straightforward challenge result in such chaos?

Chapter 2

It was Tuesday. Tuesday was fabulous because it was double P.E. Dean knew that once he had put on his kit he was 'the one', the one that every other boy had to beat. He was the player that everybody wanted on their team, the one who was sure to get a goal, the one who could channel everything he had into creating success.

When he was on the football field Dean finally felt free. He knew, of course, that there were expectations of him but he also knew that he could deliver. When he was stuck in a stuffy classroom something happened between his brain and the paper. In his mind the answers were clear, in discussions he was a key player, but when it came to having to write things down – forget it. It was like trying to play football in a pair of flippers. He knew what he had to do but just couldn't do it.

Over the years this situation had got Dean into no end of scrapes. He had, his mother said, the attention span of a goldfish – although quite how anyone was ever able to measure the attention span of a goldfish was anybody's guess. Dean had spent hours in classrooms looking at teachers, hearing a dull droning noise somewhere in his head, but not actually listening to anything. He had perfected the attentive stare, and all the time he was perfecting it he was thinking of team tactics, his last goal, his favourite premiership player, in fact anything except what he should have been doing. Teachers found him incredibly frustrating because the more alert ones had grown to realise that Dean was not listening and a typical exchange would go something like this:

'So, Dean, which of the brothers in the play do you feel sorriest for?'

'Sorry, Miss?'

'I said, which of the brothers in the play do you feel the most sorry for?'

'Well ...' A word like 'well' always gave him time to plan

an intelligent response. 'On balance ...' two more words that bought thinking time, and a pause for good effect, to make it look like you were really thinking ... 'On balance, I feel sorriest for Mickey because he has not had any of the good things in life – unlike his twin.'

The teacher's eyes would open a little and anyone could tell that she was flustered at what was a perfectly reasonable response.

'Err ...' her time to stall, Dean would think smugly. 'Yes. A good response. Anyone else like to add anything?'

Then Dean would sit back, a smile on his face knowing that, if this had been a football match, he'd just produced a fantastic tackle – a tackle that helped him save face. But it got boring. Teachers always on his back, Mum on his back when he got home, nothing ever really changing and his reports at the end of the term always disappointing. It really wasn't his fault. Now if all teachers could talk about the merits of the 4 4 2 system or whether referees should automatically send people off for diving – then he would have been all ears.

Then there were the sendings out. They were all logged on his behaviour record. Sometimes, especially when he'd been in trouble at home too, it all became too much. Why stay in the classroom when, in spite of whoever might talk next, you're going to get the blame? He'd marched along corridors full of murderous intent, refused to fill in slips, refused to apologise to teachers and he had begun to get a name for himself. Then came the reason that his mother was called in to see the Deputy Head.

He hadn't meant to call the teacher a name. He really hadn't, but he'd been in a bad mood all morning – ever since he'd opened his kit bag and found yesterday's banana had gone black and soggy and that bits of it were all over his P.E. shirt and his football boots. It was true that it was his own stupid fault, but knowing this just made everything worse.

'Dean!' Mum had yelled from the foot of the stairs.

'Hurry up, you'll be late for school.'

'Hang on will you? There's a problem.'

'Well problem or no problem, I want to see your backside down here in thirty seconds with your kit.'

'Look! This is the problem,' he said holding up his filthy sports shirt and his rancid boots.

'Well you shouldn't have put your banana in with your kit. You'll just have to borrow some stuff from school.'

'But I will get a detention!'

'Well, perhaps that will teach you.'

Glowering, Dean had kicked the pavement hard, scuffing the toe of his new shoes in the process. He normally called for Tom but today he didn't want to talk to anyone. Sometimes it just seemed as though life was out to get him. His mother, of course, had been perfectly unreasonable. He'd taken the banana to school because it was nutritional and now all she could do was moan. His eyes were fixed on the floor.

As he went through the school gates, Dean ignored everyone. He knew he'd get a detention for 'forgetting his kit' – although he didn't forget it exactly. How was he to know that a maverick banana would 'go rogue' and destroy his kit? Well okay, it would be all right after a cycle in the washing machine but nonetheless it wasn't his fault now, was it?

Marching through the front door came confrontation number one.

'Dean, please tuck your shirt in.'

'Whatever!' he scowled.

'I beg your pardon. Come back here, sort your shirt and your attitude out!'

'For God's sake! Why doesn't everyone just get off my back?'

The teacher was clearly disappointed by this response. He had expected blind obedience not a cross twelve year old who had been gently festering all the way to school and who was not in the mood to listen to anyone.

'Excuse me? I am not shouting, nor am I being rude to you.'

'Just shut up and leave me alone!' With that Dean resolutely turned his back on the teacher and went off to his locker. Of course, Dean knew that this was the wrong thing to do, but the teacher had deliberately wound Dean up. In spite of the fact that he had not tucked his shirt in, the teacher should have known how to deal with pupils like him. That's when it had happened.

He turned around and saw the teacher in hot pursuit and so he had called him a name. Now on the score of 1 to 10 it hadn't been the worst name in the world but, having already refused to do what he had been told, and having then been ruder and ruder, Dean knew he would have to face the music – and to top it all he would miss P.E.

He'd ended up in internal isolation for the day. His mother had been called (so any chance of going to football club had just evaporated) and apparently the teacher was doing something called 'a round robin' so that everybody who taught Dean could have a kick at him whilst he was down.

It was like being sent off in the cup final when you had only committed the tiniest of fouls. Life was so unfair!

Although Dean was supposed to do some work in isolation, he couldn't be bothered and sat for most of the day with his head on the desk. Now he'd have to face Mum and get the 'hairdryer' treatment. He would be made to listen without any opportunity to respond whilst she went on and on at him and then he would be sent to his room. His dinner would be delivered to his door and she'd take away his phone and his tablet leaving him stranded. This had to be the MOST boring day of his life. All because of a rotten banana and people who just would not give him the chance to be himself. Secondary school was a pain. Teachers were a pain. Parents were also a pain. Why couldn't you just push a button and suddenly become 18, just like that? It was all so pointless.

That was when, after she had collected him from school and made an appointment to come in to discuss his 'behaviour', Mum had told him that he would be going to Gran and Grandad's for the weekend.

'Can my life get any better?' he groaned sarcastically, already dreading the old fashioned curtains, the complete lack of technology and boring food.

'Well, I'm sorry Dean, but I really don't know what to do with you. Dad and his new girlfriend are on holiday for a fortnight so I can't send you there and I need a break.'

Dean felt extremely sorry for himself. Why, he reasoned, did people have children if they only wanted the good bits? Everybody is different – everybody reacts to things in different ways. I just had a bad day. Doesn't everybody?

He packed three football books and his football. At least he could kick it against his grandparents' fence – there would be nothing else to do, would there?

Chapter 3

45, Myrtle Avenue. Even the name sounded ancient. A bungalow with two bedrooms. The spare bedroom always smelled musty and Dean's grandparents never had any of his favourite crisps. By the time he arrived – at 5p.m. on Friday afternoon – Dean was feeling extremely sorry for himself. He had even cried. Not something that a man would normally do, but everyone had been so mean to him. Forced from his tablet and computer, his phone confiscated, Dean's world was pressing upon him ... and it was beige. No football team in the premiership would ever have had a beige kit – because it was BORING! It was the colour of nothing – too dark to be white and too light to have any real depth to it.

The bungalow smirked at him with its neat white fence and – oh the embarrassment! – gnomes. Who in their right mind had those maniacal little men sitting in their front garden? The beige curtains seemed to be grinning saying welcome to our beige world. You are going to be sapped of all colour and all joy during your stay ... and you'll be made to eat all of your vegetables. It was a young boy's worst nightmare. Oh his grandparents might look sweet and nice – and they smiled at his mother as she unloaded her grumpy, red faced son – but they were the enemy. And look how they dressed – everything was elasticated or knitted – the shame of it! Dean only hoped that they wouldn't take him out anywhere. To be seen with them ... he would surely die of embarrassment if anyone ever found out he'd been dispatched, given a free transfer here. Just imagine, he thought, if anyone from school saw the gnomes. His life would be over. Completely over.

It was a colourless November day – *a perfect backdrop*, Dean thought, *to the colourless weekend that lay ahead.*

Going into the front room was like going into a museum. There were photographs everywhere. It almost felt as though he were walking through history – all those eyes – people you'd never met and people you knew but in an earlier incarnation. There was his mother – she could only have been about the same age Dean was now - she looked so innocent and, in spite of the fact that she was wearing her school uniform, she looked trouble free. He could see his grandparents on their wedding day, eyes full of hope and happiness ... and something else – optimism, looking forward to the future together. And then, as he scanned further around the room, there were pictures, old looking pictures, pictures that had gone brown and a particular picture of a proud looking soldier in his uniform. Dean wondered who he was and how his image linked to the other pictures. Finally, he saw a picture of himself in his mother's arms, his father smiling at them both in the background. But, of course, families didn't always stay together, did they? Not these days, and, mused Dean, that wasn't necessarily a bad thing. After all, nobody wanted to live in a house where everybody was at war: where words became weapons and silence became a threat. No. Things were definitely better now. Well, everything apart from school.

He wondered how long it would take his grandparents to talk about the trouble he kept getting into at school. How long would it take before they tried to make him squirm in his seat, until he was forced to mutter apologies even if he didn't feel like it? He really didn't believe in apologies - they were for the weak.

Awoken from his daydreaming by his Grandfather's voice, Dean started.
'Eh there, lad, don't look like such a wet weekend. I've plenty planned for us,' and then he'd winked. This was odd. Dean was in trouble but his grandfather hadn't mentioned it. Dean ungratefully began to wonder what all of these things his grandfather had planned might be. Cleaning the car perhaps? Mowing the lawn? Being bored senseless?

'Let me take your bag to your room, lad, and then we'll go and look at the allotment, shall we?' It sounded riveting. Instead of being with his mates playing football, Dean was going to be looking at a pile of mud with some grotty vegetables.

'Where's Grandma?' he asked.

'Oh, she's gone down the road for a natter. It'll be great to see her later on, but for the time being we can be lads together.' Lads together! His grandfather was ancient.

Before they could leave, Grandad made a flask of soup. After all it was November and the ground would be grey and cold. Dean wondered what there would be to do up there at this time of year. All he wanted to do was to call for Imran and George and play football. Instead he had to accompany someone ancient to a freezing cold piece of mud.

There was nobody at the allotment. The sky was grey, it was cold enough to see your breath and there was a touch of frost on the hardened ground. Grandad explained that they had to spread some manure (Dean had wondered what the smell in the car was) and then dig in some plants that liked the cold. Garlic was, apparently, best sown at this time of year but to make sure it didn't rot they had to put a little bit of sand in the bottom of the hole. Later, they planted a particularly hardy type of pea and made sure any weeds were cleared. Dean ached for his tablet, longed for his video games – all he could see was a patchwork quilt of grey, frost rimmed mud with dead things sticking up. Riveting.

Two hours passed and, at that stage, the two retired to Grandad's shed and shared the soup. It was delicious and the time had unexpectedly, evaporated. But Dean was on guard – he was waiting for his grandfather to start to lecture him about school. The lecture never happened.

They returned to the bungalow. Grandma was still out at her friend's house so Grandad made some sandwiches which they ate in front of the television. Because Dean had not given a thought to his grandparents it never occurred to him that they had other interests and, fortunately for Dean, his grandfather's interest was football.

'Fancy watching one of those channels where you can keep up with what's happening in the Premier League, son?'

'Yea please – that would be great.'

And that's where they were when Grandma returned home with a box full of homemade cakes.

This weekend wasn't turning out so badly after all. Mum was so busy working, taking Dean to football and keeping the house clean and tidy that she hardly ever baked – and never made homemade cakes! But Dean was still suspicious.

Saturday came and went. Dinner was lovely and his grandparents seemed genuinely interested in how Dean was getting on at football. They promised to come to see his next match.

On Sunday morning, Dean went with his grandfather to the local supermarket to get some things for breakfast and to pick up the Sunday papers. They parked and went into the store. Musing in the aisles, Grandad stopped when there was a sound played over the intercom and, suddenly, like in a movie, everybody else also drew to a halt. Nobody moved. Nobody talked. Aisles were quiet. People were standing bolt upright in front of their shopping trolleys. Dean started to ask his grandfather what was going on but he, like everyone else, stood rigid and his look told Dean to do likewise. For a moment, Dean wondered if this whole scenario had been planned by his mother to make him realise that he had to behave, but then he dismissed the thought – she couldn't have involved this many people, could she?

After what seemed like an incredibly long time another

sound occurred and, without any warning, people started to move around normally again, started to talk and to carry on with their shopping. It was though they had been captured and frozen in time for the merest of moments like watching an action reply of a great goal as the ball made its way across the goal line whilst 40,000 people held their breath.

'Wow that was seriously weird? What just happened? Why did everyone stop'?

Grandad looked suddenly sombre. 'Well, Dean, it's the 11th of November, and at the eleventh hour of the 11th of November, the First World War ended and so, every year, to remember the fallen (all of the soldiers who died in that war and others since) we have Remembrance Sunday and, if the 11th falls during the week people everywhere observe a two minute silence at work or at school, so that they never forget what happened in the hope that it never happens again. So many young men went off to fight for their countries and so few returned. The First World War, which started one hundred years ago, raged from 1914 until 1919 and during that time a little under two million young men were killed. There was hardly a family in this country which was not touched by this terrible tragedy. It was an horrific war and young men fought in terrible conditions. In fact, if you look at the photographs in our front room at home, you will see a smart looking man in uniform – Company Sergeant Major (CSM) Frederick Sweeney. He was Grandma's grandfather and he was killed in a place called the Somme. Unlike many of the young men who fought who were in their teens, he was a professional soldier but he lies buried in a French graveyard and Grandma never had the chance to meet him. Apparently he was a good soldier and leader but – like so many others – he paid a terrible price.

The journey home passed in silence – not because Dean and Grandad weren't talking, but because Dean kept thinking about what had just happened, trying to process what he had just learned. He was trying to work out how the face in his grandparents' lounge was related to him. The serious looking moustachioed man in the photograph, looking proud and upright in his uniform was his grandmother's grandfather, which meant that he was his mother's great-grandfather and his great-great-grandfather. He wondered whether the soldier had been anything like he was. Had he found school difficult? Was he good at football? How exactly did he die and where was 'the Somme'? It was a bit like finding out the jigsaw that you thought was complete was actually missing a piece. He wondered what it must have been like, not for his great-great-grandfather who was a professional soldier but for those boys who, six or seven years older than he was were sent to fight at the front during the First World War and, for the first time in ages Dean Wilkins was pondering about things which were nothing to do with football.

Chapter 4

On the news that evening there was a lot of information about Remembrance Day. Sitting in front of his grandparents' old square television in their lounge, Dean watched as people dutifully placed wreaths at the foot of the Cenotaph in London – to recall the loss of life in all wars. Dean wanted to know more about it and that was how he came to stay with his grandparents for the whole of the next week. Who would have thought it? If anyone had suggested that Dean would ask to stay with his grandparents for the whole week he would have told them they were stark staring mad. Yet here he was – his curiosity piqued. He wanted to understand what had happened and he wanted to learn whether he was anything like the man whose photo looked out proudly from his grandparents' wall.

Dean thought he would ask his grandfather more about it.

'Grandad?'

'Yes, lad.'

'You know that man on the wall, the one who died in the First World War? What kind of a person was he?'

'I don't rightly know. You'd have to ask Grandma about that. See whether she still remembers what her parents told her about him. After all she wasn't born until thirteen years after that man up there on the wall had died.'

'So she never knew her grandfather?'

'No. She never did and neither did her sisters. Sad, isn't it? I bet he'd have had a grand time with those lasses. And, of course,' he said, pausing for a moment and looking thoughtful, 'there would have been many like him. Did you know that during the First World War, over two million soldiers were killed in the most terrible conditions you could possibly imagine?'

'Really? But isn't all war terrible Grandad? Was there

anything special about the First World War?'

'Well, there was something special about it. It was the first time that so many countries across the world were all involved in such terrible fighting. Men thought it would be all over by Christmas. They signed up for all the right reasons thinking that they were defending our honour. The press made it sound like a picnic and there were posters everywhere suggesting that anyone who didn't 'do his bit' was a coward. Whole villages were decimated by the death toll. It was appalling. But, from what Gran says, he was quite a joker in real life. Looks like a real stuffed shirt in the pictures though, doesn't he? I remember your grandmother telling me that many of the lads who signed up to fight on the front deliberately lied about their age so that they could join in! Doesn't bear thinking about, does it? They were just a little bit older than you, Dean, and in the middle of hell!'

All through the day there were programmes on the television about the war. Dean had never really paid attention before but today was different. Today he had a connection with it. Someone in his family had fought – and died – on foreign soil fighting so that he and others like him could stay free. For the first time he had an inkling of how people must feel when they delve back into their past to discover their family trees. He wondered whether, one day, he might be able to visit the grave of his long dead ancestor to pay his respects.

Dean's grandparents could see that he was very taken with the coverage of Remembrance Day. It was particularly important this year because it was one hundred years after the outbreak of the First World War. He looked transfixed as the images of grey battlefields loomed on the screen in front of him. He learned about the way that the men had dug trenches to keep themselves safe. They had no contact with home, no electronic devices, but in those old black and white pictures – especially those taken nearer to the beginning of the war –

they looked keen, fit and well. It was only later that the men looked haunted by a great sorrow, as though they were carrying the world on their shoulders.

Dean's mum popped by later with his school uniform and school bag. She seemed bemused by his decision to stay with his grandparents for the week.

'Well ... this is a turn up, Dean! I've brought your tablet and your phone but remember, I've got to come in to speak to your teachers this week and I don't want to hear that you've behaved badly again. Otherwise you'll lose these devices and it won't just be for a weekend! Make sure you put everything you need out the night before ... and have you done your homework?'

Homework: the challenge and curse of a school child's life. Set by teachers who, Dean thought to himself, could think of nothing else to teach you so they made you teach yourself. A complete cop out. Then came that cold feeling where Dean realised that he actually hadn't done his homework. He sat down with a scowl, spent ten minutes on each of the four subjects that were due in on Monday and did the absolute minimum required. What he wanted to do was to sit with his grandparents and ask them all about his long lost relative.

Chapter 5

One of the things Dean's grandfather had said stuck in his head: a boy of thirteen – only a little older than he was – had been sent to the front and had fought in the war. Older people have a habit of getting into a muddle, don't they? Dean was sure his grandfather must have been confused but he resolved to ask his grandmother about it.

How could someone of thirteen have dealt with the things he had seen on television? It was unthinkable. Most of the people he knew in Year 8 were concerned only about computer games, watching sport on television and talking about what they were going to do at the weekend. There was no way that a thirteen year old could have gone to the war.

In spite of his misgivings, Dean resolved to talk to his grandmother and, just before bedtime when she was making a cup of tea for herself and Grandad, he went into the kitchen on the premise of helping to carry a cuppa into the lounge.

'Grandma?'

'Yes, Dean love?'

'You know how it's Remembrance Day today and everything?'

'Yes.'

'Grandad said that your grandfather fought and died in the First World War and that he told his family that for a few weeks he had been fighting alongside a boy who was only thirteen. Do you remember anything about this? Did your mum ever mention anything like this to you?'

'You mean is it true?' Grandma hesitated as if wracking her brain to remember something she had been told a very long time ago. 'Come to think of it – that does ring a bell. Yes ... I think there was a lad who enlisted when he was only twelve and was at the front at thirteen. Doesn't bear thinking about, does it? Could be you in a year or so.' She gave a little involuntary shudder as though someone had just opened a door and she had been caught in an icy draft. 'The things those lads must have seen! I remember my mum telling me that her dad had written home and told her mother about this young lad from somewhere in London who'd been desperate to help his country and that he must have looked old for his age. Hang on … I've got a couple of the letters my grandfather sent to my grandmother during the war. My mum kept them after her mother died. I guess I then kept them all for sentimental value. Tell you what, I'll look them out if you are interested and we can go through them together. Then we can do some more searching on the internet to see whether there is any truth in it or whether it's just a bit of propaganda released to the papers to make the men who didn't sign up feel bad.'

It was hard to sleep that night. In three nights Dean felt as though someone had opened a door to another reality – one which was related to his world in some way but one which was just on the borders of truth. Someone related to him had been involved in something that the commentators on the television had called 'the war to end all wars'. Only, of course, it didn't end all wars because thirty years later there was another World War and there were more atrocities. It must have been difficult, thought Dean, for the women who'd lost husbands and boyfriends, for the mothers who had lost sons, the grandparents who had lost grandchildren and the children who lost fathers to have had any pride in what had happened given that history had repeated itself so shortly afterwards.

Looking up at the face of the soldier on the wall, Dean wondered what he would have known, what he would have seen and how he might have felt walking into what he must have known was almost certain death. If his picture from one hundred years ago could talk, what would it say to Dean? His great-great-grandson alive and well a century after he had died and been buried in some far flung corner of France?

How must it have felt waving goodbye? Dean wondered how his distant relative had coped in the muddy and bloody fields of France away from home, without television and football to play and watch.

It was getting late and Dean knew he had to get his bag ready for school. The last thing he wanted was to get into more trouble ... and that was when it happened. He was just about to turn on his heel and head to his room, when he could have sworn that the man in the photograph on the wall winked at him.

Rubbing his eyes and pinching himself to make certain that he was not imagining things, Dean put it down to exhaustion. Although he normally played football all weekend, he'd been out in the cold too long and was tired.

Settling into bed Dean realised that he was very, very weary. In spite of his inquisitive mind he was asleep within five minutes

Chapter 6

It was very dark and very cold and he was up to the top of his calves in water. Freezing water. It didn't smell too good either. Next to him a man was coughing violently and there was a dreadful smell. Dean had no idea where he was but he didn't like it at all. He opened his eyes. He could see men slumped across the walls of a deep trench. Something ran across his foot and, to his horror, he saw a huge rat ... and it wasn't alone.

A little further along the trench he could see a soldier lit up against the flame of a cigarette lighter. It was so cold the soldier was burning the seams of his shirt with the naked flame in a feeble attempt to get some warmth. There was a faint crackling sound and a smell of singeing.

Further along the trench Dean could see makeshift ladders which, had they been mounted, would have taken the men in the trench to the top and across the flat piece of land which Dean could just see when he leaned against the back wall of the trench.

As his eyes adjusted to the gloom, Dean could see that the trench was lit by lanterns and there was a roughly hewn sign reading Tattenhoe Corner. He guessed that it was to remind the men of their homes. But where was he?

Somewhere in the near distance, the blackened sky lit up with a blazing red, gold and orange flare. The noise of the explosion was deafening but, Dean noticed, very few of the somnolent men around him twitched. They were, it seemed, used to the noise. But fear lurked in that trench and it grabbed the men by their throats. It ran its sharp nails down Dean's spine, reached deep into his ribcage squeezing his heart so that it skipped several beats. Eyes tightly closed as protection against the things going on all around him, Dean realised that until this moment he had never known or understood the true meaning of being afraid. Petrified, unable to move a muscle, Dean initially thought that he was still and remaining so whilst the field all around him was being badly affected by an earthquake. Then he realised the man next to him was, in fact, shaking violently. His arms and legs looked as though they were

being shocked and that volts of electricity were violently coursing
through his veins, his sinews, his lungs, his muscles – through every
part of him. The shaking became more pronounced and then,
vaguely, Dean became aware of someone calling his name. Until that
moment he could have dismissed this as a nightmare, but now
someone in the nightmare had identified him. In the background he
could very vaguely see a man calmly caring for some of the men and
giving others instructions.

The shaking of the young soldier nearest to Dean became more
pronounced. The bitter gnawing cold gently dissipated.

When Dean finally opened his eyes, it was not the trenches that he saw in front of him but the face of his grandmother who had been shaking him gently. He had, it would seem, slept in and now had only half an hour to get dressed, showered and breakfasted in preparation for school. But Dean felt sick and disoriented. The nightmare had seemed so real. Although he was safe and secure in a wonderfully predictable world, Dean felt unsettled and afraid.

School, teachers, the football results from the weekend. All of the events which usually wrote upon the fabric of Dean's world suddenly seemed insignificant. Sitting in Grandma's car on the way to school, Dean felt his phone vibrate – it was a message from his mum.

'Make sure you don't get into any more trouble today, Dean. Speak LTR Mum.'

School had not even featured in Dean's thoughts over the weekend. He wondered when in life he had ever learned as much as he felt he had learned over the past weekend.

His homework had been done (badly) for four subjects but Dean didn't really care. He began to ponder about the boy who at the age of twelve – his age – had signed up to go to fight in the war. What was it that he had experienced last night? Was the war like that? It had been so real. But it COULDN'T have been real. It must have been a figment of his overactive imagination. But Fear had remained. It haunted him. On the edge of consciousness, but there nonetheless. A dream had him spooked – and he had tasted terror. It tasted like bile. It felt like open heart surgery – without an anaesthetic.

How would it have been possible for a boy as young as twelve to sign up in the first place? It was silly. At break time, Dean decided to do some research on this story. It must have been made up. It was impossible, wasn't it?

Dean's best friends, George and Imran, could not believe it when, at the end of maths, Dean said that he needed to go to the library. This was so unlike their friend that they looked at each other in disbelief.

'You will bro?' said George. 'I mean come on – there is no way that you would be going to the library to do your homework. Is there a special someone in there maybe?' he said, winking very obviously at Imran who laughed loudly.

'Sorry, not homework. Just something I've got to do'.

'What could be more important than break time?' sputtered Imran, amazed that Dean sounded serious. 'It's not April the first, is it?'

'Ha ha, no it isn't. Just something I need to look up.'

'What some girl's email address or, wait for it, he's going to email that new girl in 7AW on the school email system. Come on spill … we ARE mates after all'.

'Yes, you're both mates. But I am still going to the library. See you at lunch'.

'Ok, but the playground will be missing its goal scorer,' said Imran in a last ditch attempt to get his friend back. He looked at George and the boys simultaneously raised their eyebrows before heading outside.

The library was busy as usual. The librarian was surprised to see Dean Wilkins quietly entering and sitting down at one of the computers. There were a number of pupils who regularly came into the library – but Dean was not one of them. In fact when he did come in as part of a class he was usually the pupil who had to be warned by the class teacher. This was definitely out of character – there he was logging onto a computer. Several people had started to talk to him but Dean had politely sent them away and was intently searching through the internet for details on something. Moving across from her desk, the librarian was surprised to see that Dean was looking up something to do with the First World War. Perhaps he was studying this era in history, she mused before going back to the desk to help other pupils to take their books out.

Dean was transfixed. He was reading the background of someone called Sidney - a real person with a real name and a person who, according to the article he had discovered, really was only twelve when he signed up and thirteen years old when he was sent to the front line. According to what he was reading, he had signed up at such a young age and run away from home so he could do his bit for the war effort. It hadn't occurred to Sidney that he was too young. He'd enlisted only five months after he was twelve and by the age of thirteen he was fighting in France – in a place called the Somme. It was mind boggling and unbelievable.

Startled back to reality by the bell, Dean copied and pasted the article into his own file. Walking to the next lesson, he felt as though he was spending his days doing things which were completely frivolous (with the exception of his football, of course) whilst somewhere back in time someone who had been about his own age had marched into history by doing something utterly stupid but utterly heroic at the same time. In lessons Dean was no more focused. Indeed he now had more going on inside his head then before. But he was not so vocal. When he looked at his book he had written November 1914 as the date. He had to concentrate.

'Dean!'

'Yes, Sir.'

'Tell me again – what causes events like earthquakes and tsunamis?'

'Err...'

'I've just explained it. If you had been listening you would know that.'

'Sorry, I was just ... just ...'

'Just daydreaming! Get with it, please. I'm going to be asking you another question in a few minutes. If you are not listening again there will be consequences. Am I clear?'

'Yes, Sir.'

Dean knew that he needed to concentrate – not least because his mother was due to come in to school to discuss his progress – but it was difficult. He felt as though the world had shifted slightly – as though when he looked at himself in a mirror he saw someone else, not the person that he had been prior to the weekend. Then he remembered the football match in which he was due to play next Wednesday and, for the first time in four days, he moved seamlessly back into being Dean.

Chapter 7

The changing rooms were busy. They smelt of sweaty boys and sounded like a group of chattering chimpanzees, but it was the buzz before the challenge and Dean loved this feeling – the anticipation of the game to come, the banter between the boys. He knew too that the team was strong and that they had a really good season in them.

The P.E. teacher certainly shared Dean's optimism.

'Come on lads – if you work like you have done in training we can easily go through to the next part of the competition. Don't forget what we learned from the drills and don't forget that we have a cup final in us. Dean, you're the main man. You are the one that the others will turn to for leadership. Make sure that you are up for it. Don't allow tension or bad temper to destroy your game. We know the others will try to ruffle our feathers, so ignore anything they may say to you. Keep your focus on the match. It's a team game so work together. If someone makes a mistake – and everyone does at some stage – leave it and move on. Inspire, encourage, but never criticise. And Dean, it's your team once we're out on the pitch.'

The game was fast and furious. The other team were also well prepared and, at half time, the score was still 0-0. It was important to score early in the second half to destroy the hopes of the other side.

At the whistle for the start of the second half, Dean felt inspired. Clarkey passed the ball and Dean was onto it. Although the goal was a long way off, Dean noticed that the keeper was off his line and he decided to go for a long lob. He kicked the ball with conviction and watched as it seemed to hesitate in the air, stalling. It was one of those moments where you seem to be frozen in time. And then, unbelievably, the ball was in the back of the net. The other boys swarmed around Dean leaping onto him as though he was a long lost brother and the referee pointed to the half way line.

At this stage the heavens opened and within five minutes the pitch was a mud bath, and still the boys played on; all twenty two of them hungry for victory. The pitch was slippery and their kits were becoming heavily stained with mud. Just ahead the ball was spinning in a puddle on the pitch, sitting there waiting, just outside the Furzedale goal . The other side only had to tap it and they'd equalise. Dean screamed at Wellsey.

'Wellsey, make it yours. Get there!'

He felt as though his lungs were on fire as through the curtain of rain Wellsey ran like a man inspired. Dean watched as Wellsey's foot connected with the football and he dribbled it to the edge of the box, passing not one but two strikers from the other side, both keen to get the ball back and to level the score. Next in his way as he moved up the pitch was the other team's central midfielder, and he was good – a county player and on the books of the local football team. He was doggedly facing Wellsey who made a quick dink to the left and the midfielder, who made a late lunge, slipped onto his backside in the mud. Now to get the ball into the box. Wellsey's determination was fierce and would not be stilled. A great pass managed to get the ball into the zone. Dean sprinted through the heavy slippery ground before making a strong connection between his foot and the ball which saw it launched into the back of the net where the material bulged with the force of the strike. 2-0.

The lads ran over to Dean and Wellsey and within a couple of moments they were writhing in the mud. Thick mud forced its slippery way into ears, into hair, up nostrils and all over the football. The whistle. Back to the half way line again. The other team took the kick but within thirty seconds the referee whistled and it was all over. Furzedale was triumphant. But neither they, nor the other team, had ever been dirtier. And still the rain fell as though the full force of a shower were being directed down at them. It was a great day.

As he walked back to the changing room, Dean noticed his grandparents under their umbrella. He was very pleased that they had been there to watch the game and felt justly proud of his efforts.

The mud clung to his clothing now and Dean realised how cold he felt now the action of the game was over. Although he didn't normally bother, he knew that a shower was a definite requirement. Watching the dirty water flowing towards the drain reminded Dean of his dream, of the all-pervasive mud and the wet, damp smell of the trenches of his dream. He had never been more grateful to be a boy living in the twenty-first century and watching the filth from the match and the coldness he had been feeling evaporating in the steamy sweet smell of the shower.

Dean's grandparents were waiting in the foyer of the building.

'Great stuff, lad – good goal too. Takes me back to when I used to kick a ball around.'

'You played football?'

Grandad looked at Dean's grandmother with a real twinkle in his eye.

'Did I play football? Only the best centre forward Hillingdon Borough ever had – you've got to have got those genes from somewhere, eh Dean, lad?' and he winked broadly at his grandson.

'Don't listen to him, Dean. He used to run up and down the side of the pitch – hardly ever kicked the ball. I bet you've already scored more goals than your Grandad! Now let's hurry up and get home so we can get some nice warm food into you.'

It was a pleasant car journey home. Dean hadn't been in trouble. He hadn't rowed with any of his teachers and nobody had noticed how woefully poor his four pieces of homework had been. Not yet anyway – he knew it was in the pipeline but why worry about tomorrow when today was such a good day?

Sitting in the living room, after a lovely warm casserole and a cup of tea, Dean felt as though he had been wrapped in a warm blanket. He looked across the living room at the wall and it happened again. The usually dire face of his ancestor looked out at him but this time he didn't wink – he smiled!

Chapter 8

Grandad had noticed Dean's expression and he knew why the boy was confused. He didn't yet know or understand his part in the great patchwork quilt of life but he would when he had learned more about his roots and the way in which our past always informs our present.

'Dean, lad?'

'Yes, Grandad.'

'Didn't you want to find out more about that young lad who went to fight in the Great War when he was only thirteen?'

'Yes. I did find out some more in the school library because I went onto the internet. I found out that someone did go and sign up – but he wasn't thirteen when he signed, he was only twelve! Why would anyone want to go and fight? It's completely beyond me. But surely they would have realised the boy was so young.'

'Did you happen to see the picture online?'

'No, I didn't have time.'

'Well I printed it off because I thought it would interest you. Hang on a moment.' And with that, Grandad turned on his heel and headed off to his study only to return a few moments later with an old sepia printed picture of a young lad in his army uniform. Looking at his picture it was stunning to see how old he looked. Twelve? Never. Eighteen or so?

The young private looked so serious in his uniform with his smart and shiny buttons. The face didn't look afraid – he looked calm and measured but he had been to war. According to the article this young man had seen active service fighting on the Somme before being sent home. It was almost impossible to believe that such a young person could have been on the front line. Dean's grandad explained that, at time of war, once the great propaganda machine got started, men and boys felt it was their duty to protect their homeland and that a great many young men had lied about their ages so they could enlist and fight to protect their homes and families.

According to Grandad, stories about children fighting on the frontline were printed in papers but most families didn't believe what they read, feeling instead that these were lies printed to make older men feel guilty about not going to war. Grandad explained that there were posters everywhere suggesting that men who did not voluntarily sign up were cowards.

Dean felt a shudder go down his spine. How could the men who had endured such terrible conditions have been called cowards? It didn't bear thinking about.

'Anything odd happened whilst you've been here?'

Dean hesitated. His own mother already thought he was odd. He really couldn't tell his grandfather what he had seen – it would worry him. Come to think of it, it worried Dean! How could he explain that a photograph – an old photograph from almost a hundred years ago – had the power to communicate from its two dimensional surface with someone whose life was taking place so much later. Perhaps he was going down with something. That would explain it. He must have had the flu or a high temperature. Yes, that would explain the awful nature of his dream – the nightmare set in the trenches. It was weird the way that everything seemed somehow linked. The silence at the supermarket, watching the service on television, the dream with the mud and the smell and the cold, the smell of the mud at the football match and the fact that a person in a photograph – a photograph of someone who had died a very long time before Dean was born – seemed to be trying to communicate from beyond the grave.

Lost in his thoughts, Dean had not noticed that his grandfather was now eyeing him intently and was offering him a steaming cup of hot chocolate.

'Everything must seem odd. Faces on the wall …
dreams. Everything that happens, you know, happens for a
reason.'

There were words that Dean wanted to say but he could
not utter them. What had his grandfather just said? Was it
possible that he KNEW what had been happening? That was
not possible. It was pure coincidence. Everything was mad.
He needed to go to bed. Now. He needed to get back onto his
tablet and social networks. He needed normality. Perhaps this
was a dream. He put his finger into the hot chocolate – it
burned him because it was so hot. He needed the security of
his room. He needed to be alone, to be quiet with his thoughts.
But he had to respond to his grandfather.

'Odd … yes, odd. Actually Grandad, I think I have
homework to do … and I'm really tired after the football
match.

'Of course, son. I'm here though. We'll chat when you
feel more like it.'
And just like that, he had escaped to the sanctuary of his
temporary room. Dean wondered what on earth was going on
in his world. He had come here to escape from school and the
trouble which seemed to follow him around. His
grandparents hadn't plagued him, asked for details they'd just
been there. But might he, could he, be losing his mind?

In spite of the maelstrom which was Dean's mind, he fell
asleep immediately and awoke refreshed. He had almost
convinced himself that everything he had seen so far had been
a dream or that he was ill and had been hallucinating.
Breakfast was taken quickly and very soon he was walking
through the reception into school.

George had arrived shortly before Dean and they made
their way into the playground to have a kick around before
classes began. Normality seemed to have etched its way
determinedly over the crazy landscape of Dean's new reality.

Geography was boring, maths was boring, but double P.E. – with the correct kit – was a winner. As usual, Dean was the first student to be picked and he scored six goals during the forty minutes or so that he was on the football pitch. As he made his way back to the changing rooms, Dean felt as though he could have conquered anything. His confidence was sky high.

History was the last lesson of the day and this week. As it was November and because the previous Sunday had been Remembrance Day, the subject was the outbreak of the First World War. Fired up, Dean was keen to find out more about the way that history had unfolded for his ancestors and for the man whose picture was on the wall of his grandparents' living room.

He listened intently as he was told of the propaganda spread across the land by posters and by newspapers. He wondered, as he regarded the images critically, about the horrible realities that many young men would have had to face and he asked the teacher.

'Sir?'

'Yes, Dean?'

'Didn't the people who created the posters or who wrote the articles in the newspapers feel guilty that they were lying to people who went to war? And isn't it true that many of those who signed up were much too young?'

'Well, no. The people who created the posters didn't feel guilty. Neither did the reporters nor the poets who wrote patriotic verses. They were just doing a job. It's possible that once the war really took hold and men were being killed in their thousands, some of them began to feel bad, but at the beginning they thought they were helping the war effort. As regards to your other point, if they wanted to fight abroad, young men had to be nineteen years of age. They could, of course, sign up when they were eighteen but they were not allowed to be sent abroad until they reached the age of nineteen. Problem was that when they were in the army they could, at the very least, be sure of earning some money and getting three square meals a day. In addition to this, the boys who had signed up already felt like heroes because they thought that what they were doing was right. The recruitment campaigns were much more successful than people would have thought and because of this there were often hugely long queues of young men all eager to sign up. Many of them forged their dates of birth and many of them looked much older. So people did go to war when they were much too young.'

'Didn't they send them back?'

'Depends. Sometimes it took much too long to find out and, if they were really unlucky, they might have been dead before anyone realised.'

'Did they really believe that it would be all over by Christmas?'

'They did. Just goes to show how wrong people can be, doesn't it?'

Dean was thinking of the story his grandfather had told him about the twelve year old boy. He also wondered how many other young men had laid down their lives for their country believing that the most they would need to do was six weeks' training, six weeks playing heroes, and back in time for New Year. He wondered how such young men could ever have had the strength to do – and to see – what was demanded of them.

The lesson ended with homework. Students were asked to create their own recruitment posters making sure that the pictures and the words really did encourage people to sign up.

Based on his nightmare and based on what he had learned, Dean did not want to tackle the homework assignment. He felt it was, in some curious way, dishonest and dishonourable to create something which effectively lied and which would encourage young men (and older men like his great-great-grandfather) to go to their deaths. How could he go home and start to create a propaganda poster with his great-great-grandfather's eyes on him? Or perhaps he would find out today, with that very task, whether he really was going mad.

Chapter 9

As he approached his science lesson, Dean was surprised to see Mrs Grant, the Head of Year, waiting outside. She was clearly looking for someone and he wasn't too amazed when it turned out to be him.

'Dean, come along with me. We've got a meeting with your mum today. We're discussing your progress in school'.

Typical. Nobody had told him about it. The day was fast disappearing into a cloud. Lessons had been okay. P.E. had been invigorating – so much so that he'd almost forgotten about the photograph on the wall winking at him. In the other lessons he'd only been told off about five times – a vast improvement but he knew it still wouldn't be good enough for the teachers, or for his mum. Give a dog a bad name … wasn't that the saying? It certainly felt true to him. It seemed that he had a target painted on his back.

The meeting room was bright and warm. Dean's mother was already there and she was looking at a piece of paper. The Head of Year ushered Dean into the room. It was awful - two sets of eyes glaring at him, facing him down.

'Well, we know why we're here, don't we? Dean's behaviour towards a member of staff was unacceptable and he had to be given a sanction.'

Dean began to go red. Were they going to keep on about the mistakes he had made forever? He was twelve years of age. He'd made an unprompted and unguarded response to a teacher because on that particular day everything had gone wrong. Now they were going to bury him because of his behaviour everywhere else.

'And (was she really still talking?), at your request, I have done a round robin on Dean in other lessons to see if we can get a better picture of how things are going and what we need to do to keep Dean in lessons because, although he has been better and seems to be more interested in many areas, he is still being sent out far too often.'

Was it really hot in the room or was Dean being stifled by other people's expectations? It was school. In the great scheme of things school wasn't a big thing. He thought of the stern and thoughtful face of that young boy and countless others who had gone off to war. Calling a teacher a rude name and being sent out of lessons was irrelevant, wasn't it, when compared to that?

Mum was looking upset and muttering something about his having been sent to his grandparents' for a while, and Mrs. Grant was nodding as though she completely understood. It was enough to make your blood boil. Dean knew where this was going. Report. He'd be put on report so that he was accountable to every teacher in every lesson. He'd had enough.

'Right, from Monday you will go on report,' said Mrs. Grant far too smugly, thought Dean.

Naturally his mother was going to agree. She always did. He knew that if his back was really up against the wall she'd be on his side but he really didn't get why everyone made such a big thing about school. He knew his dad had always been in trouble when he was younger and he'd still got a job. He watched their mouths moving, knowing they were talking about him, and it all went completely over his head, like dandelion seeds blowing in the wind.

Suddenly, a word blasted its way into his consciousness. Homework? Yes of course he would be doing homework – the thought of the poster loomed large in his head – even if he utterly, completely disagreed with what he had been asked to do.

The meeting had only taken about twenty minutes but Dean had felt as though his feet were stuck in mud and that he was surrounded. There was only one way out and that was to capitulate – to give in to everything that was being said. He felt like a coward but this was survival – it was all part of a game and one that he knew the rules of.

To his horror, as they left the meeting room, Mum patted Dean on the back, hugged him and gave him a kiss on the cheek before thanking Mrs. Grant for her time and effort. What was worse was that big mouth Maguire was in the corridor at the same time and had seen it all. Sometimes being a school kid was a nightmare, thought Dean, but then, just for the briefest of moments, in ten seconds of suspended time he realised that his real nightmare had shown him what horror really was, and suddenly Maguire's future taunts seemed to disappear. What were words after what he had seen?

Packed back to class, Dean was glad he wasn't going home this week and in the pit of his stomach there was a feeling somewhere between excitement and fear. When he got home he was going to man up. He was going to sit down with his A3 piece of paper and he was going to produce a propaganda poster.

Chapter 10

The evenings were drawing in now that winter had her long claws out. Going across the room to draw the curtains for his grandmother, Dean remembered he needed to do his homework.

Having played football after school, bathed and eaten his supper there was no way to escape the inevitable.

As if reading his thoughts, Grandad said 'Any homework tonight lad?'

'Yes I have, but I don't really want to do it.'

His grandfather put his head to one side and regarded Dean carefully.

'What's the problem?'

'I just don't agree with what I have been asked to do.'

'And what is that?'

'Well, in our history class we are studying the start of the First World War. We learned about the way the government of the time made sure that enough men signed up. You know how we were talking about that really young lad who forged his date of birth? There must have been lots like him and so many of them died. Yet the posters made out that the people who didn't sign up were cowards and that they were letting their side down. They made them feel as though they weren't really men at all and ... worse than that ... some of the posters made out that going to war would be a big adventure. But I think ...' he paused because, for the second time that day, someone else was eyeing him intently. 'I think that it was actually a nightmare, like we said. Like when you told me how many people were killed. It doesn't bear thinking about. So how can I really create a recruitment poster?'

'Well, why don't you do something different?'

'Like what?'

'I don't know something that shows something else – an anti-recruitment poster from later in the war, from a soldier's

point of view, maybe?'
Did Dean really see the soldier on the wall nodding and looking down with a wry smile?

'And if you get in trouble just tell them you discussed it with Grandad and this is what you decided to do.'

This made a great deal more sense to Dean. It would be truer to his feelings and his poster would be different because it would be realistic. The reaction of the teacher, well, that was an imponderable – but at least he had his grandfather on his side and that gave him a feeling of strength. What he could not explain, however, was the sense of affinity he felt with the man on the wall. He could almost sense that man's fierce sense of injustice. It was as though his reactions to things were being judged by someone who had died a long time ago. A trickle of anticipation wove its way down Dean's spine and danced, for the briefest of moments, in his mind. This poster was going to be a statement.

Feeling he had something to prove for all of the voices that were so horribly stilled during the First World War, Dean let the pencil work hard on the paper beneath his hands. It felt almost as though the pencil was propelling itself and after about half an hour he winced as he looked at what he had drawn.

It was the trench from his dream. As he looked into the picture the men were standing in foetid, dirty water in which rats were swimming. Their faces were thin, grey and tired. The picture was in black and white and there was no sign of colour anywhere. It was a grim image. One of the men was crouching in the bottom of the trench even though it was thick with water and he looked completely terrified, traumatised by the sheer hopelessness of it.

Across the top Dean had written:
Sign up now and enter the hell that is war: There is no heroism in war – only regret.

Dean's grandparents stood transfixed at the image.

'Well son, it's certainly a statement is that,' said his grandfather proudly. 'It looks like the kind of images we now see in books and photographs about the First World War. Did you know that many of the men who died did so because they fell ill rather than because of enemy fire?'

Dean hadn't known this but looking at the bleakness of the picture it was not hard to believe.

'What gets me, Dean,' said his grandmother, 'is the way that your picture looks so real. You must have spent ages looking at photographs!'

Before he could answer, Dean looked at his grandfather who was staring at him intently and, Dean thought, knowingly.

'I'm just going to get those old letters that I talked about the other day,' said Dean's grandmother, quickly returning with an old brown box tied up with string.

'My grandmother passed them to my mother who, in turn, passed them to me. Your great-great-grandmother lived to be a very old lady, but she never forgot her husband and that is why she kept his letters. I think she also felt it to be important that the stories of men who fought on the frontline were kept alive so that they served as a kind of warning to future generations in the hope of preventing the same horror happening again.'

Dean could hardly concentrate. He was desperate to read some of the letters inside the aged box to learn more about history – his history.

Looking at the scribbled and stained page in front of him, Dean suddenly felt as though he were reading someone else's diary – it was uncomfortable. Except that this diary was connected to him because someone whose genes had probably in some distilled way filtered down to him had been somewhere horrendous and he had taken the time to impart some of his experiences to his family.

The first letter had been written when Dean's great-great-grandfather had just arrived. It was tense but optimistic. Reading it aloud for the first time in about one hundred years made it sound strange and displaced out of time. It also seemed odd, though, because Dean was imagining that he could hear the voice of the man who had written.

We've arrived at the front – thank goodness for that, because that means we will all be home soon. The men are in good spirits and tomorrow we are pushing on. We haven't seen any action so I am hoping that it stays this way. Please do write – it really helps to keep up my spirits as when I read your words I imagine being in the lounge with you and our Ronnie.

All my love Fredrick x

Dean wondered how many details the letter writer had kept secret from those he loved. He looked up to the face on the wall above his head. The soldier stood bolt upright – it was a proud and patriotic stance which told anyone looking that he was proud of his country and everything that he and his uniform stood for.

Seeing her grandson looking up at the author of the letter, Dean's grandmother said 'Oh Dean, why don't you take a picture of my grandfather into school with you? You can show the other students what a real soldier of the time looked like and, if you want to, you can copy out the words from his letter. You can show them something that really does date back to the time you are studying – something which makes it all that much more real.'

It would have been difficult to go off to war, Dean thought to himself. Trudging for miles and hauling equipment wasn't his idea of fun. He'd sooner have been down the football field outmanoeuvring the other team, creating and scoring goals, becoming a hero in his own lunchtime. The men who went away to war had to give all this up. Some of them, as he had learned, were still really young. They must have missed home.

'Grandma?'

'Yes, Dean?'

'I can't imagine missing football and roast dinners. Do any of your grandfather's letters explain how he coped?'

'Well, strangely enough, there is one dated Christmas 1914 which talks all about a game of football.'

This was odd. How could anyone have written about football when he was in a dug out trying desperately to remain alive? Dean looked perplexed and rubbed his head. 'But how did the men have time to play football when they were always looking out for the enemy?'

'This match was against the enemy,' his grandmother explained, smiling at her grandson. 'Even in the middle of the most dreadful moments there are times when people do the strangest and most marvellous things.'

Digging into her bag, she looked through a couple of old fragile looking letters.

'Aha! Here it is,' she said triumphantly. 'Read this and then we can chat about it.'

In front of him were two rather crumpled and muddy pieces of paper. Almost too excited to start reading, Dean had to calm himself down before he could actually decipher – and take in – what he was reading.

My darling Irene,

I am so sorry not to have been home for the celebrations but with a little luck it shouldn't be too much longer. Our dug out is freezing cold (particularly when it rains or snows) but we have managed to make a number of small fires which provide a little warmth.

Christmas Eve was very memorable and cold just like at home. Some of the lads suggested a game of football. At about ten o'clock in the morning, one of our men started to shout. He could see a German heading for us – but he was unarmed. Behind him were another two men. At first, we thought we ought to shoot them but then it became clear that they just wanted to wish us a happy Christmas. Completely unbelievable!

It brought home to me the madness of war. Officers and men from both sides helped to bury the dead. In war nothing is as you think it will be.

The next thing I knew someone had lain down some garments at one end of 'No Man's Land' and someone else laid down more at the other end and they had made makeshift football posts. That was how the game of football came about. Not that I like to boast, but I did score two goals. Sadly our German counterparts were more skilful and, in spite of our best efforts, we lost 3-2. I do hope this is not a predictor of the outcome of the war!

It was like being in a movie. Nothing made sense. I am much older than the rest of the lads and it was genuinely moving to see them all shaking hands and playing in such high spirits. Christmas carols also echoed around the trenches. I do hope this war doesn't go on for too long. It all made me miss home even more – I longed for a proper roast turkey with all the trimmings.

I have, of course, heard some stories about some casualties, but here's hoping that I will be home soon sitting in the lounge with a bottle of stout and a willing audience.

All my love,
Your ever loving husband,
Frederick x

'What do you make of that then lad?' said Grandad, who had been standing behind Dean, reading over his shoulder. 'Beggars belief doesn't it?'

'It does. Did this really happen? I mean, why would you play a game against people that just a day or so earlier you had been trying to kill?'

'Goodness knows. I guess the pressure of the situation must have got to all of them. Many of them were just boys really. Imagine sitting in the pitch darkness never knowing when a shell was about to hit – it must have played havoc with their nerves. Also, imagine coming face to face with someone just as young as you and knowing that it was kill or be killed. It's really hard for us, in this day and age, to imagine how terrifying it must have been. Many of those lads had never been out of their homes, and here they were, not even knowing if they would ever see the people they loved again. Although your great-great-grandfather doesn't mention it in his letter home, by this time (and we were only four months into the war really) 40,000 people had already lost their lives. He and those around him would almost certainly have been haunted by things that we can have no concept of.'

The black and white poster stared up at Dean. He glanced up at the picture on the wall just in time to see the man in the uniform unmistakably mouth the words 'thank you'. With a little cry Dean fell back into the armchair. Fortunately, his grandmother had just returned to the kitchen but his grandfather was studying his face hard.

'Catches you like that doesn't he?' he said before turning on his heel. Moments later, he returned with a copy of the photograph on the wall.

Dean's mind was in a turmoil. Where did reality begin and end? Was he going mad? He rubbed his eyes hard – something was definitely wrong. Pictures couldn't talk, dreams weren't real and his grandfather could not really have had any clue about what was going on. Feeling an arm upon his shoulder, Dean turned around. 'Feels strange? Think you're going barmy? Seeing things that could not possibly be there? Don't you worry lad – you aren't going loopy!' He turned to face the soldier on the wall. 'The old man chooses who he communicates with. When we first moved into this house – a very long time ago now – it was me. I was having problems at work and all I can say is … well, he usually communicates with people who need it.' He smiled gently at his grandson. 'Don't worry your marbles are intact. But don't say a word to Gran – she'd never understand, and he is her relative after all so she'd feel a bit odd if she knew he only communicates with us men, don't you think?'

Was this for real? Dreams had somehow become totally lucid – so much so that you felt as though you were awake when you weren't. Looking at his grandfather's face Dean pinched himself hard. It hurt. He was not dreaming. The world was getting crazier. For a moment he wondered whether he should go home – but that might appear rude. His grandfather held out a photocopy of the soldier's photograph and Dean, without really looking at it, consigned it to the top pocket of his blazer and then promptly forgot where he had put it. It sat next to his pictures of United and his report card and faded from his memory as easily as a rainbow when the rain stops.

The inner conflict of wanting to ask his grandfather about what he had just said but also wanting to pretend everything was normal meant that Dean was unusually quiet – and yet his grandfather said nothing more. Dean almost convinced himself that it had been his imagination playing tricks again before he decided (unwillingly) to do his homework. He'd already been in trouble for the poor pieces of homework he'd done earlier. In his head he knew, of course, that he had not put in any effort, but it was still a shock to be asked to repeat them. Never mind, on this occasion they would keep his brain occupied and that wasn't a bad thing at the moment.

Once the homework had been done and supper had been eaten, Dean realised he was actually much more tired than he had thought. So many ideas and thoughts were racing around in his head at the moment. And so it was that no sooner had he lain down upon the bed he had almost fallen asleep ... until, that was, he heard a voice. It was coming from his blazer pocket.

Chapter 11

'Dean! You're not going mad. It's just my job to make sure that you know when to fall into line,' the voice was saying. When he opened his eyes, Dean felt as though he was an extra in a film. He was with a group of men all of whom were sitting around reading letters from home. The man closest to him, however, was scribbling in a notebook. He seemed intent. Dean didn't need to wonder where he was – he knew. What he didn't know was how far into the war they were.

Moving closer to the man scribbling in a diary he saw an inky scrawl saying 1918. He also saw roughly drawn sketches of a gas attack – he knew this because at the top of the page in larger writing were the words 'Gas! GAS! Quick, boys!'. Beneath the words were hellish pictures of men struggling to get their gas masks on. Realising that he was now very close to the man, Dean moved back a little although the man was, it seemed, completely oblivious to his presence so absorbed was he in what he was doing. The text on the page was neatly laid out in lines and every now and again words had been crossed out to be replaced with other words and occasionally several options seemed to have been tried before the initial word was reinstated. It looked like a poem. Dean knew that he was due to be studying the poetry of the First World War in school and wondered whether this man in front of him had produced anything memorable or whether he – like so many others – would do anything for a bit of escapism to get away from the horrors he had seen or had yet to see. What this sad, defeated looking man didn't know was that the war would be over by that November. And that his own battle would be over a little before that. Permanently.

Rubbing his eyes, Dean moved slightly and almost fell out of bed. Had that brief interlude been a dream? Like before, it had seemed so real but it couldn't have been. He fell back into a blissful slumber dreaming of running up the wing, taking on the last defender and scoring the winning goal for

England.

It was Wednesday. The worst day of the week. The day that featured all of Dean's most hated lessons. A feeling of gloom descended upon him like a heavy mist. |t was almost as though he were walking through a jungle of doubts and concerns.

The day did not go well. There was too much going on in his head. In the first lesson Dean was caught doodling in his book. In the second lesson he was sent out into the corridor. In anger he kicked the wall.

'You can give that a rest for a start!' a familiar voice shouted loudly. Although he looked all around there was nobody in the corridor.

'Have you no idea who's talking, lad?' The voice sounded different from the teachers who usually plagued Dean's days. 'Pull those shoulders back. Be a man!'

It was coming from his top pocket. But that was not possible. What should he do next? Dean reached into his top pocket, rifled through the documents and pulled out the picture of Company Sergeant Major Sweeney. He looked dour and critical and it looked as though he was about to talk again. Dean wondered what a breakdown felt like. Was it like this? Was it where reality seemed to be an indeterminate vague entity? If so, then he, Dean Wilkins, was definitely going mad.

'No, you're not going mad. Didn't you hear what your grandfather said to you? You know lad, you only get out what you put in. Most of my poor lads who are now pushing up poppies in France and Belgium would have given anything to have had the opportunities that you and your lot have now. Imagine being eaten alive by lice – men had to use naked flames to burn their eggs from their clothing because the itching was driving them wild. Even on the bitterest of nights you would see lads doing this.' That explained what Dean had seen earlier in his first 'visit' to the trenches. The voice continued. 'Then there's respect. You have to follow the line of command or nothing gets done. You might want to yell all kinds of abuse but you can't. You have to keep a lid on it, boy. Get those shoulders back – take pride in yourself. You owe it to all of us.'

Great! Somebody he had never met, somebody who had died years before he was born was now playing the 'guilt card'. Dean scowled to himself just in time to see Imran, who was in the class opposite and who had spied him through the window, waving to him. Sometimes being out in the corridor was a whole lot more entertaining than being in the lesson. Today, however, it sucked.

'And you can take that look off your face!' said the voice again.

Angry, Dean reached into his pocket and crumpled up the photograph.

The teacher who had sent him out came into the corridor to talk to Dean about his attitude. In spite of feeling as though he was in a reality television show, Dean managed to remain focused and polite. He apologised for his rudeness and promised that he would return to the lesson to complete his work.

'Well done,' remarked the voice from his pocket. Dean wondered whether the teacher had heard this and perhaps misinterpreted the remark as rudeness, but Mr. Jones gave no indication whatsoever of having done so.

Instinctively, Dean pulled his shoulders back and ignored George who was desperately pulling faces to make him laugh. George's attempts became more obvious and, whereas Dean would normally have got into trouble by laughing at his friend, this time it was George who found himself despatched to the corridor. It was also George who was seen making faces into Imran's classroom and George who lost his break. Dean smiled inwardly.

'See,' came the voice from his pocket. Nobody else had responded. It would seem, mused Dean, that he was the only person who could hear the voice of his great-great-grandfather.

The last lesson of the day was English. They'd read a play about two brothers separated at birth. They had also read a book about a family who helped Jewish children to escape from the Germans in France and today, it seemed, they were going to be studying some poetry from the First World War.

Normally this would have been accompanied by a groan – after all boys and poetry, thought Dean, just do not go. Now give me an autobiography of a Premier League Football manager or ask me anything about football stadiums and players and I will be up for it. Dean Wilkins – my subject of choice is the Premiership from 2012-2014. Now, these things would all have gained and retained my attention in normal circumstances, thought Dean, but the poetry of the First World War was a fascinating subject. How could anyone capture in words the horrors of the trenches, the conditions and situations those men found themselves in? He wondered about the man who he had seen so intently focused and scribbling words and images into his notebook. Had his words ever found their way to a publisher? Would he have known if they had? It was all so fascinating.

The class began with a little bit of a history lesson and a discussion of the way in which the writing from the beginning of the First World War was deliberately upbeat whereas the poetry from the end of the war was much darker, more sombre, more realistic. Dean remembered the page he had seen, and the date – 1918. So the poem he had seen being written by the grey and very sad looking man would probably have been negative.

Then the teacher showed a picture of one of the most famous poets from the First World War. Dean instantly recognised the sad face staring out at him from the interactive whiteboard at the front of the classroom. He could see a man with a middle parting and a thin moustache – the very man that Dean had seen so intently leaning over his notebook. Dean's world was becoming more and more confusing. He wondered what was so amazing about the poetry of the period that it should continue to exist so many years after the War but suspected that he was about to find out. Teenage boys generally find poetry about as interesting as classical music and Dean was no exception. When, over the years, his teachers had started to talk about rhyme and rhythm and all sorts of strange things, Dean had simply disconnected. In his head he was usually worrying about whether a 4-4-2. system would work against the team that he and his schoolmates would be playing in the County Cup Final and trying to look at his phone under the desk to get the latest news about the latest 'transfer window'. What interest could poetry ever have for someone of his age?

But today was different. He stared at the man on the whiteboard – remembering the intent concentration on the young man's face as he had been hunched over the stained notepad and the way in which he had scribbled out so many of his own words. He also remembered something about gas being written across the top of the notebook.

The teacher explained that today's 'Key Question' was: What did the poets of the First World War hope to be able to convey through their poetry?

It felt as though he – Dean Wilkins – was being asked to justify why people like the morose young man would spend his time writing down words.

When he heard his own voice offering an opinion, Dean's football ideas dissipated more quickly than rain on a hot summer's day

'Do you think that soldiers wrote poetry as a form of escape from what was going on all around them?'

'Stupid answer! It was so much more than that,' came a voice from his pocket.

The teacher showed no signs of having heard the man's voice but instead of making any comment about the opinion Dean had voiced, she asked him to hand out a poem written by 'the late and great Wilfred Owen' and having read it to decide whether he (or anyone else in the class) would like to change his opinion.

Dean and Imran were looking at the poem together. It was a description of men marching across the battlefield. The words chosen by the poet were clever. Dean felt as though he could almost see the men hunched over and marching in a straggly line as shells exploded behind them. The men in his mind were so weary that they were unable to react to what they were hearing and their feet were covered in blood. But then, Dean saw the lines which stood alone. 'Gas! GAS! Quick boys!', and he felt as though he was suddenly sitting beside the poet. The line he had seen scribbled at the top of the page marked a moment of panic in the poem.

'Why does the poet talk about gas like that?' Dean asked.

'Because the gas that the Germans used was noxious and it destroyed eyes and lungs and caused great pain,' said the male voice in his pocket.

'Dean, it's because the mustard gas caused terrible suffering to our men. It was a chemical weapon and the men had to carry gas masks at all times to try to protect themselves. But if they couldn't get the masks on in time the men suffered and died horribly. Owen describes watching someone die,' explained his teacher.

It was amazing. Dean felt invigorated. The poet had wanted not to send a silly and romantic view of life in the war but to tell the people who were left at home exactly what happened to men on the front line. He had wanted to show the suffering of ordinary soldiers. It felt as though Dean was on the same page as the poet – he had created anti-war posters for homework. Suddenly poetry didn't seem so inconsequential. Suddenly a meeting that could not have possibly have occurred, and about which he could tell no one, had changed everything for Dean – he'd been lucky enough to have had just a glimpse into hell. He had not lived it but had felt it in a way that nobody else could have done. It felt weird. And now, in spite of the fact that all of these thoughts were completely crazy, Dean felt that he must immerse himself into the lesson.

Finally, students were asked to write their own war poems. They were all given a folder. In the folder they were able to read a diary entry from a soldier in the trenches, a report on mustard gas and some optimistic poems that were written at the beginning of the war. They were then asked to write their own poems based upon the difficult conditions in the trenches and on the battlefields.

'Go for it Dean,' came the familiar voice from Dean's front blazer pocket. 'You've got more insight than the others. Think about what you are learning about the conditions that the men had to endure.'

The voice no longer worried Dean because it was obvious that he was the only one who could hear it. In a way it was also strangely comforting and it made him feel as though he had a vital link with the past.

Time, it seemed, had begun to accelerate because no sooner had Dean started to write the poem than he found he had finished. He read through his words and they described in detail the smell of the thick clinging mud, the cold of the water that ate into the men's bones as they sat shivering in the trenches. He had written about the desperation of men burning the eggs of lice from the seams of their shirts and the terrible noises in the background which punctuated their suffering.

At the end of the lesson, Dean gave in his poem and he never expected to hear any more about it.

In history he gave in his 'alternative' poster – the poster that suggested the nature of suffering. And then, without another thought, he, Imran and George headed for the football pitch at break.

Chapter 12

Imran was fast – he 'nutmegged' Dean and made him angry as he ran quickly up to the makeshift goalmouth. *He* was the best footballer and Imran had made him look like a donkey. In haste, and without thinking, Dean kicked out. Deep down he knew that he was acting rashly and Imran fell heavily spraining his ankle and screaming in pain. George ran to get Matron leaving Dean waiting with his victim, feeling the heavy weight of responsibility. He'd deliberately fouled Imran and it made him feel miserable now that Imran was writhing on the floor in front of him. What was worse, the team had the County Cup next Wednesday, and if Imran's ankle wasn't any better by then they'd have to use either Jonesy or Wilko, and neither of them were any good. It would be like playing with ten men – and it was all his fault.

The only saving grace was that his blazer had been left on the bench miles away so he wouldn't get any grief from the voice in the pocket. Listen to me, Dean thought, there is something seriously up with the way I am thinking. Every time something happens, I check myself and wonder what someone who has been dead for almost one hundred years would say about it!

Fortunately, Imran's ankle was badly sprained and not broken. Unfortunately, however, a sprained ankle was unlikely to mend by next week. Imran seemed to think that he had been hurt because of a badly timed tackle and not because Dean was suddenly and irrationally insanely jealous. But Imran was wrong.

'Disappointing lack of discipline you showed there lad. In the War all men looked out for each other all the time. I was a Captain and my lads were like family to me. I would never have dishonoured any of them and yet you – in peace time – do that. Unbelievable! You've learned about the football match that was played on Christmas Eve, haven't you? Do you think those lads, many of them under the 19 years of age they were supposed to be and in the middle of a terrible war where they were seeing their friends die horribly, took advantage like you did with that lad today? And he a friend of yours! Remember, lots of those boys died for you to have the chances that you have today. You're letting them down and selling yourself short.'

It was bad enough that he had to deal with his own guilt, now he had another critic. How was it that suddenly everything he did was observed? Dean had never felt more ashamed. He looked down at the ground in front of him and it swam before his eye. His head felt hot and heavy and nothing made any sense. That voice in his blazer pocket was bugging him too. Nobody needed a conscience sitting on their shoulders 24/7. When would it stop? Should he go back to Mum's before the end of the week? However, Grandad had suggested that *he* had also communicated with the soldier – with Frederick - and that was a conversation that he needed to have with him. Dean needed to find out whether he'd imagined his grandfather telling him that. In the meantime, he needed to learn to take responsibility. He realised that he really needed to learn how to handle his anger so that he didn't take it out on someone else. The voice was right. What right did he have to behave like this?

The rest of the day's lessons went past in a blur. There was only one thing that Dean wanted to do and that was to talk to his grandfather. Was his grandmother in on it too? It hadn't seemed that way. Who would have thought that their beige little house, complete with gnomes, could house such a secret? Why had all this happened at exactly the same time that he had been studying the First World War at school? Also, as the war had started one hundred years ago – the fall out was inescapable. Dean had watched the television transfixed as someone had poured red poppies from one of the windows in the Tower of London to signify the deaths of all of those who had lost their lives in the First World War. Seeing 800,000 ceramic poppies pouring out in a never ending stream helped Dean to have a greater understanding of the price paid by so many men. His grandparents had watched in silence – there were no words to describe what they were seeing. It looked as though the very building was bleeding. It made Dean think of the blood that must have been spilt on foreign fields and of the families who would have gone to bed every night praying for the return of their loved ones – often for loved ones who would never make it home.

His great-great-grandfather, Frederick Sweeney, at forty years of age and a professional soldier, had lost his own life out there in France and Dean wondered how, as a soldier in a position of authority who was effectively leading young men to their deaths, he must have felt every time one of his men was killed or injured. Hearing his voice (or something which appeared to be his voice) helped to put things in perspective. Usually things like this on television would simply have washed over Dean. He would have 'switched off' and sought refuge in an electronic game or he would have been sharing some banter with his mates either on a social networking site or by text, but although he kept hearing his phone ping he had ignored it. There was a gradual dawning of the difference between the ages. Time might have come down like a veil over the years but the price paid by those who had fought in the war must never be forgotten. He realised, ashamedly, that many young men not much older than he was had never had the opportunity to return to the country they loved, to watch their siblings grow up, to argue with their families, or to simply enjoy playing football. Imran had taken the brunt of Dean's frustration just because he had shown him up on a football field, but those men he was learning about had always looked out for their mates in situations that were the fuel of nightmares. From what he had read in class, Dean had learned that even those who returned had been plagued by recurring nightmares in which the horrors they had seen revisited them at random times. Sometimes their screaming would awaken whole houses as 'the terrors' would grip them and, for a few moments they would find themselves back in hell. Other times, a sound – a car backfiring in the middle of the day, for example – would reduce them to quivering wrecks. Worse still, Dean had learned that some of the men who had been so traumatised by their experiences had run away from battle and, once caught, they had been shot as 'deserters' by the very country that had driven them to the precipice of madness.

But there was a conversation to be had. It was Thursday tomorrow and Dean would have to go back home at the end of this week. He needed to understand what was going on.

An opportunity presented itself after supper as Grandma had to go out to visit a friend leaving Dean and his Grandfather alone in the house. Dean had already done his homework and phoned Imran to see how he was feeling.

Grandad was sitting in his armchair with a steaming cup of tea and reading the paper. He had, however, been regarding Dean over the top of the pages and could see that his grandson was keen to have a conversation.

'Go on then, son – ask'.

Dean was startled. His grandfather had an unerring ability to pick up on his feelings. He didn't really know where to start. What if he had imagined the signs? What if he had imagined the fact that Grandad always looked at him 'knowingly' and that it meant nothing? Perhaps he had imagined those few times his grandfather had suggested that he knew more and that the conversations with the man on the wall and experiences in the trenches he thought he had been having were all merely figments of a very fertile imagination. His mother had always told him that if he had been able to harness his imagination he'd have been a genius. Musing was taking a lot of time and his grandfather was still looking at him like an inquisitive owl. His newspaper was lowered and his glasses sat oddly on the end of his nose.

'Shall I start then?' asked Grandad. 'Since you came to us, you've been seeing and hearing and dreaming things that could not possibly be. You aren't sure who to talk to ... because if you choose the wrong person they will think you are crazy. The man on the wall – C.S.M. Sweeney – is related to you. He, as you know is Grandma's grandfather, your mother's great grandfather and your great-great-grandfather. None of us ever had the privilege of even meeting the chap and yet, somehow, he seems to be able to communicate with some of us. We can even hear his voice and nobody else can. It is exceptionally strange.'

Dean's mouth didn't often drop open but it did now. His grandfather had described the situation perfectly. When he did speak again his words would not link into sentences.

'Yes ... but how? What? It doesn't ...'

'That it doesn't ... but it still happens nonetheless. I'd lived here for twenty years with your gran and I was getting into trouble at work all the time. If I saw that something was wrong I'd say so – didn't care who I spoke to and didn't think before I spoke. I just blurted out my thoughts without any kind of screening. It got me into trouble. In fact, I almost lost my job – twice – and, according to me, nothing was ever my fault. It was always the problem of the management. I hadn't learned to take responsibility for my actions. That's when it started to happen. Of course, I was so tied up in my own ideas and self-importance that I really couldn't see the wood for the trees. I had been sent home from work early. The boss said that I needed to re-think my 'attitude to work' and that if I couldn't see it had been wrong he wasn't sure that there would still be a place for me. I was furious – almost called him a name that I would have regretted, stormed out and slammed the door. I drove home too aggressively, sounding my horn at each and every person who had the misfortune to get in my way. When I got in, I sat here in an extremely bad mood. Gran wasn't due home for a couple of hours and I didn't want to talk to her or to anyone else. Then *he* looked at me and gave it to me with both barrels. He told me that Gran deserved a husband who would look out for her and basically told me to start to look at things in a more responsible way. Initially, of course, I thought I'd gone stark raving mad. I thought the boss had caused me great stress and that I could sue him for mental cruelty. And then *he* – Frederick Sweeney there – taught me what mental and physical cruelty was really all about. That night I had the most vivid dream I'd ever had. I was in the trenches in 1915. The war had been raging for a year and it certainly wasn't the 'game' that people thought it might be. I saw young soldiers – much younger than I was – having to put up with what could only be described as hell on Earth. Of course many of them couldn't handle it. But there, in his uniform, just like he is in the picture – a fine figure of a man, nearly forty years old – was your great-great-grandfather Sweeney. It was his job to keep his men together. He didn't really say very much but he opened my eyes to the importance of listening to that little voice inside that suggests to you that you know you're being wrong and unfair.

I went back into work and apologised. Never again did I challenge the order of things without thinking first. Of course, I'd always give my opinion if asked but I was respectful. I'd hear the CSM's voice in my ear if I started to deviate. It happened all the time for a while. Then it stopped and never returned. I think I had learned by then. So you see Dean you're not going mad. Most people would never believe you if you told them, but there's a reason why you can hear the things you are no doubt hearing and there's a reason why you are seeing the things that you are no doubt seeing. What happens next, well, that's up to you, but, that smart and proud soldier up there won't want your mum to suffer because she is his great-granddaughter. He'll be looking out for her too. And you, you are his great-great-grandson, which is why he is trying to help you. Having his photograph on the wall is a way of making sure that we are always connected to our own history, a way of knowing that there is a link between the blood that was shed by CSM Sweeney and the blood that is coursing through Grandma, your mum and your own veins at this very moment! Your stay here came at a very good time. You might have noticed I never once asked you how or why you were getting into trouble. I just had a feeling that someone else would do it for me – and in a much more effective way than I could. Does this make sense, lad? I don't think I've ever known you to sit so quietly for so long!'

Of course it made sense – but then it didn't make sense either. Dean couldn't really put words to how he was feeling. This whole experience had been more than strange. He wondered if one day in the distant future *he* would put the picture of Frederick Sweeney into a frame and might it talk to his own children. But that was mad, he thought, he was only twelve years old. But so had that young lad been when he did the unthinkable and signed up to go to the bloodiest battle he could ever have imagined.

'Grandad?'

'Yes, son.'

'Have you ever been out to see Frederick Sweeney's grave?'

'I have. It's in a little corner of a place called 'The Somme' in France – just opposite a working farm. There are rows and rows of headstones, all most beautifully kept. I think it's important to take the time to visit these places. They are always quiet, respectful and peaceful. When I went I almost felt that I could hear the voices of the men who had died, but then again that probably was my imagination. You should ask your mum to take you there.'

Dean felt an overwhelming urge to ask his mother to do just that – but he knew he had to bide his time. Perhaps he would have an opportunity to talk to her about this when he told her about the fact that he had been studying the history of the First World War at school and then he could tell her that Grandad had told her about her long distant relative Captain Sweeney who had lost his life in that very War.

Dean's thoughts were interrupted by the sound of his grandmother's key in the lock. Granddad winked at him and so did the picture on the wall. But they didn't need to. Dean would never tell his grandmother about the things that he and his grandfather had discussed. He had learned so much this week but it was up to him to put it into action.

Chapter 13

Friday morning came and Dean went into school as normal. Today, however, he did feel different, more grown up really – it was hard to explain.

In history he was surprised to see his poster next to the whiteboard. The teacher – who was, of course, usually on Dean's back – was probably angry, he thought, about the fact that he had chosen to write an anti-propaganda poster rather than one which told of the potential glories of warfare.

'Dean?' said Mr. Jones. 'I am just about to start the lesson but I wanted to ask you about your homework.

'Yes, Sir.'

'Why did you choose to create a poster that was so different from everyone else's?'

Dean felt embarrassed for a moment but then he thought back to his nightmares. He also remembered the information in the envelopes that he had been given in the English lesson.

'I just felt, Sir, that with all we have learned in our different subjects – and on the television – that it was wrong to glorify war. It was apparently 'the War to end all wars' and yet a few decades later we were at it again and more men suffered and died. And from what we have seen, the First World War was terrible, the men – and they were mostly young men – really suffered.'

Remembering the importance of lines of command, Dean knew that, should he continue to disagree with the teacher, he would need to be respectful and so he hesitated before answering.

'Well I think your poster is excellent, Dean. That's why I have chosen to display it at the front of the classroom. Your images are terrifying as are the expressions upon the faces of several of the men who are in the trench. It almost feels as though you were there and able to see, and to understand, how some of those men were feeling. I also really like the words and language that you have used at the start and that is why I have placed this poster here.' He paused and smiled at Dean. 'Sometimes it's really important for people to think beyond the literal, to question what they are being told and to look beyond the obvious. In my mind that's exactly what you have done here and it's impressive and – to be honest, Dean – it's a lovely surprise. Your homework is usually hurried and poor but this clearly took you a long time and you have every right to be proud of yourself.'

It felt as though, from inside his front blazer pocket, Dean's great-great-grandfather was tapping him in pride. That feeling – that emotion – was not something that Dean Wilkins usually associated with school. The eyes of the class were upon Dean and not because he had shouted out, disobeyed instructions or given someone a nasty foul – it was more like he had scored a hat-trick against a Premiership side and it felt good.

'Bloody hell!' whispered George. 'I never knew you were going to turn into a spod – mind. Even I have to admit it's pretty sick – wish I'd done it. Is that what living with your grandparents does? Perhaps I'll ask my mum if I can stay with mine. Only problem is, they are in Scotland – that, and I don't think they like me very much.'

Later on in the morning it was English, which was always a potential problem for Dean because he simply could not keep quiet and his frustrations were usually vented in comments like 'For God's Sake!' or 'Course it's only me who's talking, isn't it?' and, of course, a stubborn and downright refusal to accept his part in anything. In the previous lesson the class had been studying the poetry of the First World War. They had looked at sources from the time and eventually had to write their own poems.

Once again Dean's poem was chosen for special consideration to be read to the class. The teacher was amazed at his 'creativity' and 'powers of imagination' which, she felt, really brought the horrors of trench warfare to life. She had, she said, even telephoned his mother to tell her how happy she was with his work. Imran and George were making faces at each other across the classroom. They started to mouth words to each other but they were noticed.

'George! Imran! Perhaps you would like us to read your poems out. Or, looking at them, perhaps not. You can both stay behind after the lesson and we will have a discussion about the importance of paying attention to your learning. You know, you only get out what you put in.'

At that stage, the teacher had chosen to read Dean's poem to the rest of the class. Dean listened carefully. He could not remember writing a single word – he must have been writing on automatic pilot. But the words and images that he was hearing reminded him of all that he had seen, heard, smelt and read. The acrid smell of burning as shells exploded somewhere behind the dugout. The stinking, foetid mud and the unmistakable metallic tang of fresh blood. He remembered the riotous fat rats which seethed at the bottom of the trenches and the flesh torn by continual scratching because of the lice which infested the men in the trenches. Then there was the bitter cold, the freezing weather, the trenches up to a foot deep in water and the crying and incessant shaking of some of the lads. And there, just on the edge of memory, a shadowy figure – a figure he could now recognise – it was Company Sergeant Major Sweeney of the Cheshire Regiment, the man who had been there for most of the War before he too had been killed in an enemy field hundreds of miles away from those he loved and who loved him. A man who would go on having an effect as long as stories about him continued to be told and as long as he was able to find people who needed him. With pride Dean remembered that it was this man's blood that now ran in his veins.

When his mother picked Dean up that Friday, she was

excited to see the son about whom she had received not one but two positive phone calls from teachers. Thank goodness that meeting with the Head of Year had done some good. But there was something different too and it was difficult to say exactly what it was. Dean seemed much calmer much more serene than the boy who had flown so badly off the handle because of the revenge of the banana on his P.E. kit.

'How's football?'

'Fine. We had one match and Grandma and Grandad came to watch. The final is next week, except Imran's hurt his leg so it will be difficult for us to win.'

'Difficult but not impossible. You've got to believe that you can win.'

'Yes, you're right. I think even with Wilko or Jonesy we have a chance.'

'What? No argument? You okay?'

'Yep. You know that we have been doing about the First World War in school? I wondered whether, during the summer, we might be able to go across and see Grandma's grandfather's grave. Apparently it's on somewhere called the Somme. She has shown me a map of the place and the plot where my great-great-grandfather is buried.'

'You mean my great-grandfather?'

'Yes.'

Dean's mum was surprised. He had never expressed any interest in her family tree and here she was having been called by two teachers about a poster and a poem that her son had created. Dean had never put his creative mind to such good use in anything other than football before now and so she felt duty bound to agree given the fact that, at last, she would be able to have a conversation which was not about the transfer window and whether such and such a referee was mad as well as blind.

'I guess we could. I'll find out from Granny and we'll see if we can pay our respects this summer. I was thinking of taking you two boys camping to France anyway so we will need to take our car over. It would be an adventure, wouldn't it? Might teach Joe something too.'

Chapter 14

The following year in July, Dean, Joe and their mother made the trek to France. After much studying of the map they found the graveyard in a place called Bronfay Farm Military Cemetery in a tiny area called Bray-Sur-Somme. As his grandfather had said, it was very peaceful. The dappled afternoon sunlight fell across the grass and made the carefully planted flowers seem vibrant in the heat. The only noise came from the far off sounds of a combine harvester and a dragon fly as it hovered nonchalantly in the air close by. Just beyond the walls stretched acres and acres of cornfields. The whole scene was so idyllic that it was almost impossible to believe that it had once been a place of carnage – a place where there had been nothing but miles and miles of freezing mud with skeleton trees in black and white, the whole scene had once resembled a negative. There had been barbed wire and suffering. The graves, silent and stark, were reminders of that. Each carefully carved memorial stone had the name and the age of the soldier beneath it. Sometimes, Dean noticed there were up to half a dozen men from the same battalion, all of whom had died on the same day. He tried to imagine the man who had been in charge of these young soldiers – a man like his great-great-grandfather – and the great sorrow that would have been created by the loss of so many. He tried to picture the faces of the people at home in England when they received the dreaded telegrams telling them that the hope in their hearts was in vain. He felt hot salty tears as they began to stream down his cheeks and fall upon the rich earth beneath his feet.

Closing his eyes, Dean realised that his grandfather was right. You could almost imagine that you could hear the voices of the men buried beneath the turf. He reached into the pocket of his hoodie and squeezed the now rather crumpled photograph of his ancestor. He felt at last that whatever lay ahead held no terror for him, that nothing would ever feel quite the same and that, should he ever have children of his own, he would make absolutely sure that, wherever he lived, he would have a copy of the same framed photograph of Frederick Sweeney that adorned his grandparents' wall. He also felt strangely calm reflecting that sometimes, although things can appear to be impossible, connections and the influence of those who have travelled this way long before us, can continue to influence what we choose to make of our lives today.

Author's Note

Frederick Sweeney does indeed lie buried in the Bronfay Farm Military Cemetery on Bray-on-Somme. May he and all of the rest of the fallen rest in peace.

Printed in Great Britain
by Amazon